Brian Wildsmith

The Hare
and the
Tortoise

OXFORD
UNIVERSITY PRESS

A hare and a tortoise were having an argument.

The hare, who could run very fast, thought he was much

The Hare
and the
Tortoise

For all children, young and old.

OXFORD
UNIVERSITY PRESS

Great Clarendon Street, Oxford OX2 6DP

Oxford University Press is a department of the University of Oxford.
It furthers the University's objective of excellence in research, scholarship,
and education by publishing worldwide in

Oxford   New York

Auckland   Cape Town   Dar es Salaam   Hong Kong   Karachi
Kuala Lumpur   Madrid   Melbourne   Mexico City   Nairobi
New Delhi   Shanghai   Taipei   Toronto

With offices in
Argentina   Austria   Brazil   Chile   Czech Republic   France   Greece
Guatemala   Hungary   Italy   Japan   Poland   Portugal   Singapore
South Korea   Switzerland   Thailand   Turkey   Ukraine   Vietnam

Oxford is a registered trade mark of Oxford University Press
in the UK and in certain other countries

British Library Cataloguing in Publication Data
Data available

ISBN 978-0-19-272708-4 (paperback)

1 3 5 7 9 10 8 6 4 2

Printed in China

more clever than the tortoise, who could only move
slowly and had to carry his house around on his back.

But the tortoise did not agree. To the hare's surprise the tortoise challenged him to a race. 'We will run from here, over the hill, through the hedge, then along the carrot field to the old cart,' he said. The hare laughed. 'I am *sure to win*, but we will race if you like.'

News of the race spread quickly,
and the birds and animals
gathered to watch.

'The tortoise will not have a chance!' cried the fox.
'Wait and see,' said the owl.

The cock offered to start the race. The spectators stood
back, and the cock swelled up ready to give the signal.

'Cock-a-doodle-doo!'

In a flash the hare was off,
flying over the grass.
The tortoise had hardly moved.

In a few moments
the hare had run
over the hill and
reached the hedge.
He looked behind,
but the tortoise
was not in sight.
The hare stopped
to nibble some
tasty leaves.

The tortoise plodded on,
and came to the hill.
It was hard work
for him to climb it,

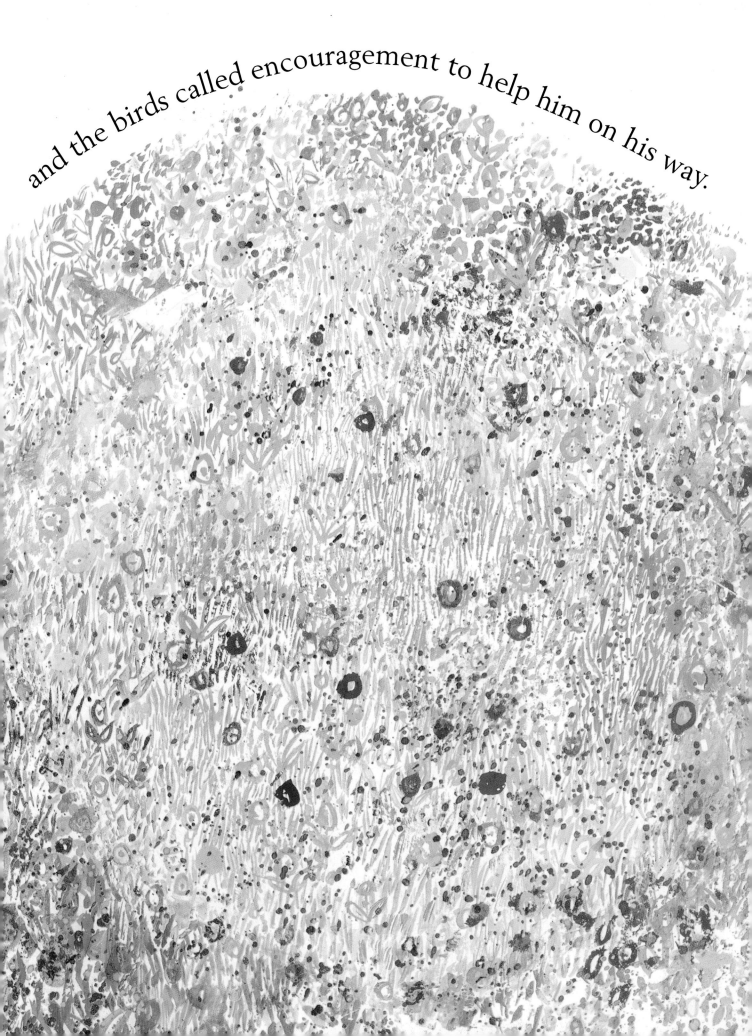

and the birds called encouragement to help him on his way.

The hare had finished eating the leaves in the hedge and dashed off again at full speed to the carrot field. He was very fond of carrots and *could not resist* stopping to eat some.

He ate and *ate* until he was
so full he had to lie down
and sleep for a while.

The tortoise had only just reached the hedge.

He was already tired, but kept walking slowly on.

At last he reached the carrot field, but the hare was *too fast asleep* to notice him passing by.

Suddenly the hare woke up. He stared in astonishment towards the old cart, the winning post.

The

tortoise

was

almost

there!

The hare
ran as fast
as he could

but it was no use –
the tortoise had
won the race!

All the animals gathered round the tortoise while he told how, in his *slow and steady way*, he had won the race from the *quick and careless* hare.